find what's WACKY

PRESS

Los Angeles · New York

Especially for Kamran

Written by Steve Behling
Interior design by Laurie Young
Cover design by Stuart Smith
Image retouching by Sherry Spence

First Edition
Printed in the United States of America
10 9 8 7 6 5 4 3 2 1
12102014-D-2
ISBN 978-1-941341-28-5
Visit dreamworkspress.com

BEST FRIENDS!

Years have passed, and Hiccup has proven himself to be a dragon expert. Together with his trusted friend Toothless, the last of the Night Furies, they explore their world in search of new dragon. Explore the pictures below, and see if you can find all 5 differences.

You can turn to page 42 to explore the answers to this puzzle!

AWESOMENESS IN ACTION!

Astrid is an incredible dragon rider and a spirited warrior. She and Hiccup ride their dragons, Stormfly and Toothless, into unbelievable adventures. *Your* unbelievable adventure? Spot the 3 things in each of these three pictures that are different from the original below.

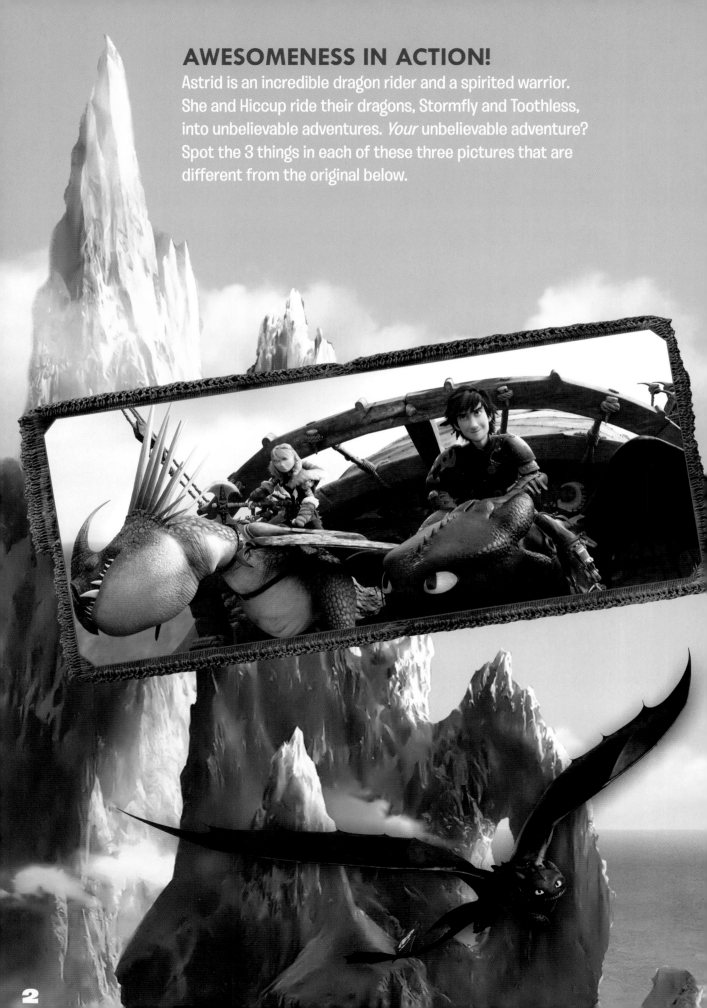

You know what isn't unbelievable? The answers to this puzzle are on page 42!

FOLLOW MY LEAD!

Hiccup's dad, Stoick, is the leader of Berk. He has mellowed a bit since the Vikings made peace with the dragons. See if you have the leadership skills to find all 5 differences in this picture!

Turn to page 42 to find the answer to this puzzle.

MAKING THE CALL!

When the people of Berk gather, it's always a big scene! See if you can find all 6 things that are wrong in the big scene below.

You don't need to have your own dragon to fly on over to page 42 to find the answer to this puzzle!

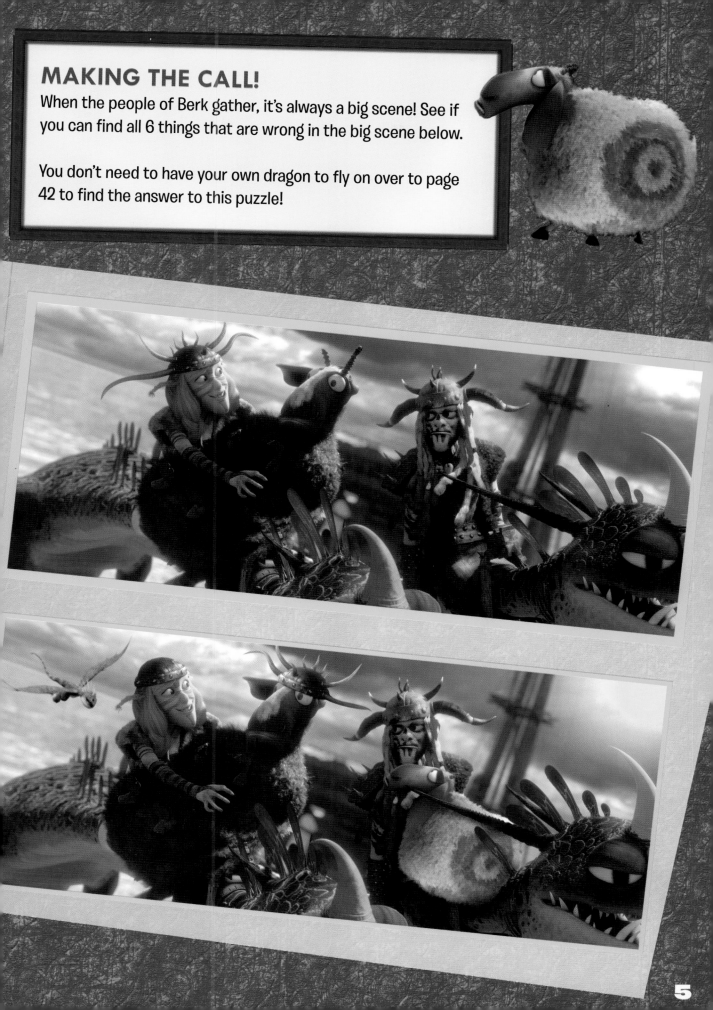

DON'T MESS WITH DRAGO!

Meet Drago Bludvist, a madman on a quest to steal all dragons. Here he faces a mysterious stranger. Now it's your turn to face off against a friend of yours. Choose either Player 1 or Player 2 and compare your image to the original. Whoever finds all 6 differences first wins.

Don't mess with the puzzle answers either! Turn to page 42 and you'll find them there.

Player 1

Player 2

MYSTERY REVEALED

Who is the mysterious stranger pictured below? Look no further than to your right—it's really Hiccup's long-lost mother, Valka! Taken by dragons years ago, she is now their fierce protector. Protect your reputation as a dragon master by finding all 5 differences in each of these sets of images.

Does a dragon master need to look at the puzzle answers? Probably not...but it couldn't hurt! Turn to page 43.

SNOTLOUT... STRIKES!

Snotlout soars through the skies on his Monstrous Nightmare dragon, but this time he has a buddy. You won't need a buddy to solve this puzzle, though. See if you can find all 3 differences in each of the three pictures to the right.

Don't be *sheepish*—you can find the puzzle answers on page 43!

DRAGON STABLE!

Have you ever seen so many dragons in one place before? Probably not. (And if you have—that's awesome!) Now it's up to you to search the image below and find the 6 differences from the original image. Get flying—dragons await!

You don't want to get burned—turn to page 43 for the puzzle answers!

TEAM RUFF AND TUFF!

Ruffnut and Tuffnut are back, and these twins mean trouble. They're all about danger. And so are you! Dare you brave the danger to find the 1 image that matches the original one below? Good luck!

Puzzle answers are like a two-headed dragon.
We're not sure how, but turn to page 43 anyway!

GOBBER AHOY!

Gobber's taken to the high seas, along with Astrid and Eret. If you can find your sea legs, then maybe you can also find the 8 things that are different in the image below.

Some people get seasick, but no one gets puzzle-answers-sick. Turn to page 44 for yours!

Player 1

TAKE WING!

When Hiccup and his mom, Valka, soar into the skies atop their dragon friends, you know that action awaits! And action awaits you and a friend. Choose either the Player 1 or Player 2 image, and see who can find all 8 differences first.

Player 2

Take wing to page 44 to snare the answers to this puzzle!

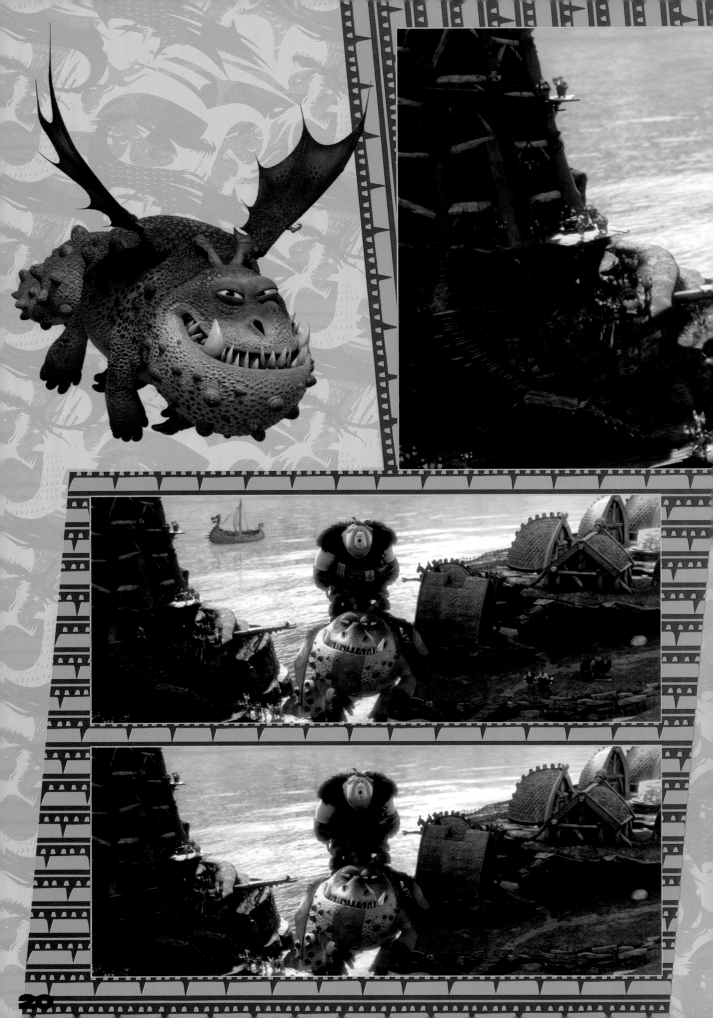

FISHLEGS IN FLIGHT!

Fishlegs is a bit of a dragon nerd. There's nothing he doesn't know about his flying pals—even the Gronckle! See if you can help the big guy identify the 3 differences in each of the three duplicate pictures.

If you want to know everything there is to know about the answers to this puzzle, turn to page 44!

21

DRAGONS ASSEMBLE!

Hiccup's surrounded by his dragon friends, including Toothless and Stormfly. Surround yourself with this image below, and see if you can spot the 9 changes that were made to the original picture.

Don't stare at this picture too long, or you might get seasick! If you need help, turn to page 44 for the puzzle answers.

SURROUNDED!

These Vikings could use your help. Eret, Ruffnut, Fishlegs, Astrid, Tuffnut, and Snotlout are surrounded. And you're surrounded by six images—and only one is the same as the original! See if you can identify the 3 changes made to each of the other images.

Psssst! Turn to page 45 and you'll be surrounded by puzzle answers!

...eam Drago's on the move—his men are on the march and his dragons have taken flight! Stop him from accomplishing his evil goals by finding the only image on this page that is different from the image below.

March on over to page 45 for puzzle answers!

STRIKE FROM THE SKIES!

Hiccup and Toothless lead an amazing array of dragons into battle. Now it's your chance to take the lead as you search for the 8 differences between the original picture and the duplicate below.

There are dragons everywhere,
and there are answers to this
puzzle on page 45!

DRAGON DIFFERENCES!

Here's a puzzle with a twist. Check out the first picture of Hiccup, then look at the other image. See if you can spot all 8 things that have been added to (or removed from) the original image! If you can, consider yourself a true dragon master!

You can still consider yourself a true dragon master even if you check out the puzzle answers on page 45!

READY FOR BATTLE!

While Hiccup, Astrid, Gobber, and Stoick gear themselves up for battle, it's time for you to do the same with your friend. Each of you will choose to be either Player 1 or Player 2. See who can find all 8 differences from the original picture, and you'll be the ruler of the skies!

Player 1

Player 2

Gobber says you should check out page 46 if you want to know the answers to this puzzle. Listen to him—he means business!

AIRBORN ASTRID!

When Astrid takes to the air, who knows what will happen? And who knows what will happen when you try to find all 3 differences in each of the duplicate images on this page. The sky's the limit!

There's no limit to what you can discover by checking the puzzle answers on page 46!

TOOTHLESS TELLS IT ALL!

Toothless uses his mighty dragon mouth to deliver a message to Valka and Hiccup. Meanwhile, we've got a message for you: find all 8 differences in the picture below. Come on—all of Berk is counting on you!

You can count on us to give you the answers to this puzzle—just turn to page 46!

BEHOLD THE BEWILDERBEAST!

Hiccup, Valka, and the heroes of Berk have an enormous dragon called a Bewilderbeast on their side. But guess what? So does Drago! Who will win in this epic battle? And who will win the epic battle between you and a friend as you choose either Player 1 or Player 2 to see who will be the first to spot all 9 differences?

Bewilderbeasts are awesome, but it's *not* awesome to be bewildered! Turn to page 46 for the puzzle answers!

Player 1

Player 2

HEROES TO THE END!

Every epic battle is won by heroes, and the fight between Drago's forces and the heroes of Berk is no exception. Face your final battle by finding the 11 differences in this image, and know that you're among the finest heroes Berk has ever seen!

Even a true hero needs help from time to time, so if you need some—just turn to page 46 for the puzzle answers!

1
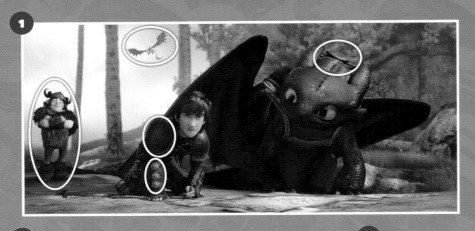

3

4

5

6

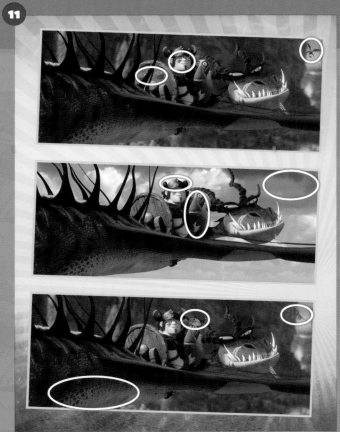

16

18

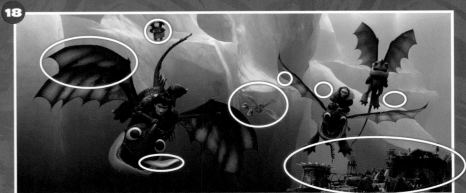

20

22

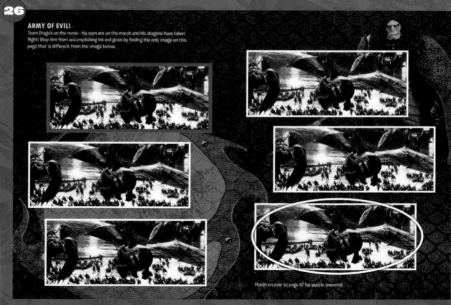

26

ARMY OF EVIL!

Team Drago's on the move—his men are on the march and his dragons have taken flight! Stop him from accomplishing his evil goals by finding the only image on this page that is different from the image below.

March on over to page 47 for puzzle answers!

30

ANSWERS

33

36

35

38

40